Angel Academy

Musicals and Messages

D0988211

Janey Louise Jones

USBORNE

"Oh, she sounds lovely. I wonder who will get the role of Angelica!" said Gabrielle, half to herself.

"I would love to be the star!" exclaimed Ruth.

"Same here!" said Hope.

"Me too!" said Merry dreamily.

"Yes, it would be nice," said Gabrielle, realizing that quite a few girls were keen to take on the starring role. It was such a shame that there could only be one Angelica.

First published in the UK in 2014 by Usborne Publishing Ltd.,
Usborne House, 83-85 Saffron Hill, London EC1N 8RT, England.
www.usborne.com

Illustrations by Antonia Miller.
Illustrations copyright © Usborne Publishing Ltd., 2014

The name Usborne and the devices ♀ 🎈 are Trade Marks of Usborne Publishing Ltd.

A CIP catalogue record for this book is available from the British Library.

JF AMJJASOND/14 ISBN 9781409538639 02787/1
Printed in Chatham, Kent, UK.

Chapter 1

Gabrielle Divine adored her life at Angel Academy. She loved everything about the school, from its fairy-tale castle appearance – complete with curving white stone walls, dreamy turrets and inspiring courtyards – to its very special lessons.

It was the second half of the spring term at the Academy on Cloud Nimbus. Gabrielle and her friends had just completed the

Vanishing Skills Charm, which meant another charm for their bracelets and another step along the path to becoming Guardian Angels. The Head Angel, Madame Seraph, was so proud of the Cherubics for winning their latest charm that she had awarded them a special treat. It was Saturday – and she was allowing them to go to the new Sparkles cafe in Bliss, the town at the heart of the angel world.

"I think I'm the only one who's never been to Sparkles!" said Gabrielle excitedly as she brushed her shoulder-skimming chestnut hair. She was sitting at her dressing table in the Crystals dorm, trying to decide what style would look best for the cafe trip – loose with a soft curl, or a topknot? She shared the dorm with her three angel friends, Ruth, Hope and Charity. The others had all visited the cafe in the Wintervale holidays, but she'd spent the holidays with her parents back at home on earth.

"You are *so* going to love it!" said Ruth. "Everything in there…well, sparkles! The cakes, the teacups, the waitresses' outfits! In fact, I'm going to sparkle too and wear a sparkly ribbon round my ponytail!"

"In that case, I think I'll wear my hair loose with sparkly hair clips!" said Gabrielle, smiling at her best friend.

"And I'll wear my sparkly beads," said Hope, rummaging in her velvet-lined, musical jewellery box.

"Okay, I'll wear my sparkly earrings!" decided Hope's twin sister Charity. "The ones I got from Granny last birthday."

"Yes, they're so pretty," said Hope. "One of Granny's better ideas! I wish she'd given them to me – I got that scratchy scarf instead."

"This is such fun. Let's go completely sparkle-crazy!" said Ruth, as she applied a generous smear of silver glitter eyeshadow to her eyelids with a little brush.

"Erm, I think that's already happening!" giggled Gabrielle.

Angel gowns, angel wings, angel charm bracelets and angel halos. The angel world *never* stopped delighting Gabrielle, who had been living at the school for only a few months. As she took her favourite spring dress from her wardrobe, admiring its soft lilac folds and the

shimmering pearls
and sequins stitched onto
the detailed bodice by Angel
Willow, the sewing mistress, she felt a
sudden wave of happiness. She belonged
here now.

Gabrielle was soon ready but her room-mates were still dithering over which dresses to wear, so she wandered towards the window which overlooked the lovely gardens. On the windowsill an exquisite pink and silver dove, named Sylvie, sang contentedly. Sylvie carried messages for Gabrielle and her Crystals room-mates, and was like a kindly auntie to all of them.

"You look lovely!" chirped
Sylvie, as Gabrielle stroked
the little bird's head.

"Thank you, Sylvie. The lilac *is* pretty, isn't it?" said Gabrielle.

As she gazed out at the grounds, Gabrielle thought about how much Angel Academy felt like home now. It was amazing how quickly she'd made new friends here, and they already meant so much to her.

"Come on, Gabrielle, stop daydreaming!" said Ruth. "It's time to go!"

Gabrielle spun round with a smile. "Oh! You all look gorgeous!" she exclaimed, admiring the dresses they'd chosen. Ruth was in lemon, while Hope wore powder blue, and Charity had plumped for pale pink.

"Has everyone got their sparkly stuff on?" chirruped Sylvie.

"Yes!" chimed the girls.

"Then have a lovely time."

"Sparkles cafe, here we come!" cried Gabrielle, as the Crystals girls floated excitedly out of their dorm.

The centre of the town of Bliss was a lovely little hub of market stalls and small shops, selling everything from chocolate and jewels to perfumes and trinkets. Gabrielle had visited Bliss a few times before but she never stopped being amazed by the pretty place.

The four friends landed softly outside the Sparkles cafe and Gabrielle gasped with wonder as she took in its shimmering window display. It was filled with glittering cupcakes, ribbons and bows, and china teacups galore. "It looks so…*delicious!*" she said happily, clapping her hands with glee.

They floated inside and Gabrielle's eyes grew even wider as she spotted a rotating glass cabinet filled with delectable pink cupcakes, some decorated with iced rosebuds, others with glittery icing, and yet more with pearls and edible jewels. They all looked much too good to eat. "These are incredible! Like works of art," said Gabrielle, feeling almost as if she was looking into a jeweller's cabinet.

She sat down with the others at a large round table, making sure to keep spaces for Merry and Fey, their friends from Silverlight dorm, who hadn't arrived yet. As they waited, the girls began to chatter about one of their favourite topics – charms. Earning charms was the goal of all the pupils at Angel Academy. Each charm they gained showed that they'd achieved one of the skills needed to become a Guardian Angel. And the two little charms which spun and dangled daintily from the exquisite bracelet she'd been given on the first day of term reminded Gabrielle that she was making good progress.

"I can't wait to start work on the Messenger Charm," said Gabrielle.

"Same here," agreed Hope.

"Yes, carrying messages is something we'll have to do a lot of when we're Guardian Angels," said Charity.

"I know. I can't wait to go to earth and help humans," said Ruth.

"There's nothing too exciting about earth!" said Gabrielle. While all her friends were from the angel world on Cloud Nimbus, Gabrielle was half angel, half human, and she'd lived with her parents on earth until starting at Angel Academy just a few months ago.

At that moment, Merry and Fey arrived.

"Hey, Merry," said Gabrielle. "Isn't it gorgeous here? I love it!"

"I knew you would," said Merry, sounding a little breathless. "I'm glad you've seen it at last."

"You seem a bit out of breath," said Gabrielle. "Are you okay?"

"Yes, I've been rushing, that's all. I'm dying to tell you something! We had a bit of news just before we left the dorm," said Merry.

"Oh, do share!" said Ruth, who loved nothing more than gossip.

"Well, we've heard that Madame Seraph is going to announce something really fun to all the Cherubics later on this afternoon!" Merry exclaimed.

"Really?" said Gabrielle. "We didn't hear that. What could it be? We don't usually get announcements on a Saturday."

"It must be the school show!" said Ruth, bouncing up and down and grinning from ear to ear. "It *has* to be!"

"Yes, that's what Larissa's big sister said. But we don't know what show it will be! If the older angels know, they've been sworn to secrecy." Merry turned to Gabrielle. "They must have told you when you first came to Angel Academy that the Cherubics put on a show for parents to watch at the end of the spring term. It's one of the highlights of the year."

"Oooh, now you've said it, I think it was mentioned, but with so much going on recently I'd forgotten all about it."

"Yes, it has been a bit crazy already this term, hasn't it?" laughed Ruth, glancing at the twins.

Hope and Charity looked at each other rather sheepishly. They'd had a big falling-out over the last few weeks, but were now best sisters once more.

"I'm so intrigued," said Gabrielle. "I'd love to be in an angel show. What could be more special?" Her mind was already conjuring up images of show-stopping dresses, glamour and sparkle!

"It's so exciting!" said Hope. "Who'll be the star, do you think? Oh, I wish it could be me…"

"I wish I knew what show we're going to do," said Charity. "Then we could start preparing."

At that moment, a gorgeous angel waitress with glittery white wings and wearing a pretty pink dress arrived at their table, offering up a china cake stand with the most mouth-watering cakes Gabrielle had ever seen. For a moment she forgot all about the school show as she tried to decide which to sample first. And the others quickly got lost in choosing what to eat too.

Gabrielle lifted the dainty silver fork beside her plate and tried a piece of her chosen cake: a vanilla and rose-petal cupcake.

"Mmmmm, delicious!" she said. "It melts in the mouth! I wonder how it's made? I'd love to take the recipe home to Mum. We could try baking some in the holidays."

"I've never made a cake in my life," said Ruth.

"Really?" said Gabrielle. "You don't make cakes at home? Mum and I always bake at the weekends. Well, *used* to."

"Oh, that sounds nice – your mum's so lovely," said Ruth. She'd met Mrs. Divine on Parents' Day, when Gabrielle's winged horse, Domino, had brought Gabrielle's parents from earth to visit Angel Academy.

"She is," agreed Gabrielle, pushing away a sudden moment of longing for Mum, who she hadn't seen since Christmas. She took another bite of her cake and focused on the fact that hopefully she'd be seeing both her parents again soon – when they came to watch the school show.

As the girls chatted and nibbled, they discussed what the show might possibly be. And soon enough, the cakes were eaten. It was time to get back to school and hear what Madame Seraph had to tell them.

They could hardly wait!

Chapter 2

Angel Fleur was waiting for the Cherubics when they arrived back at Angel Academy.

"Please go directly to the school hall, girls," she said. "Madame is going to make a special announcement."

"Today is just too exciting!" said Gabrielle, dying to know what the show would be.

The Cherubics sat near the front of the

big school hall on sumptuous purple velvet seats and waited for Madame Seraph to appear – which she soon did. She hovered above the girls, looking as majestic as ever, her bright blue eyes sparkling and her golden hair lit by a shaft of sunlight.

"Girls, I am sorry that I couldn't share this news with you last night during our regular announcements," she began. "There was still much to decide. But here we are now and I will get straight to the point."

Everyone was so keen to hear what Madame had to say that there was utter silence. Gabrielle thought she could hear every heart beating in the school hall.

"As many of you are aware, it is an Academy tradition to put on a Cherubics musical production in the spring term –

and this year is no different. I am thrilled to announce that in a few weeks' time our Cherubics will be performing...*Angelica!*" The Head Angel beamed.

Cheers filled the hall, and showed no sign of dying down as Madame smiled patiently. Gabrielle could tell from the fantastic reaction that the choice was a popular one but, as with many things in the angel world, the story was not one she'd even heard of.

Eventually, Madame Seraph held up her hand for silence and, once the girls had calmed down, she continued. "I know we all love the story of the brave little angel whose purity and light shine through even though she has no parents to guide her," she said. "There are many excellent roles in the story, and some wonderful songs, so we felt it was the best choice for Angel Academy's annual Cherubic show. A list of parts will soon be produced and brought by messenger doves to each Cherubic dorm. Angel Fleur will also issue audition sheets with trial sections for each character – these are what you will need to prepare if you would like to audition for a main part. There will be extra singing classes available from next week, while Angel Lara's music club will be heavily involved in the production too. Auditions will be held next Friday in the school theatre. Good luck!"

The hall was filled with an excited hubbub as the young angels all began chattering at once.

Madame held up her hand for silence

once more. "And girls," she said, "I know you will all be excited about this and will do your very best – but if at any point a teacher feels that the show is interfering with a Cherubic's main schoolwork, that pupil will be excluded from the show. Do you understand?"

The girls nodded.

Madame dismissed the girls and disappeared; a babble of excited chatter followed.

"I've always loved that story!" said Hope.

"Same here," said Ruth. "My granny used to tell it to me almost every night when I was little."

"I always wanted to *be* Angelica," said Merry, sounding wistful.

"I've never actually heard of Angelica before," Gabrielle

admitted. "I'm sure she's amazing but I don't know the story."

"Oh, sorry!" cried Ruth, giving her friend a hug. "We should've explained. She's this sweet little orphaned angel who takes on the world all by herself. She's really adorable – and very brave."

"Oh, she sounds lovely. I wonder who will get the role of Angelica!" said Gabrielle, half to herself.

"I would *love* to be the star!" exclaimed Ruth.

"Same here!" said Hope.

"Me too!" said Merry dreamily.

"Yes, it would be nice," said Gabrielle, realizing that quite a few girls were keen to take on the starring role. It was such a shame that there could only be one Angelica.

Chapter 3

The girls floated along to music club later
that afternoon.

"The songs in *Angelica* are so lovely!" said
Hope. "I know all the words. We used to
listen to them all the time at home." And
she began singing some of the lines from
the main songs in the show: "All Alone",
"Mercy", "Dreamin'", "Honey Buns" and
"Family Now".

As the others joined in, Gabrielle listened carefully. "I can't wait to learn them," she said, trying to memorize some of the words.

In the music department, Angel Lara seemed as excited as the Cherubics. "Girls, today, we're going to run through some of the songs from *Angelica*. I have song sheets for you all, and I shall accompany you on the piano," she explained. "From now on, I'll be running some extra singing classes and, for those of you who would rather play their instruments, I'll be forming an orchestra to perform the music for the show. It's a busy time! And you will all have to work extremely hard. But it will be such fun. Oh, girls, do enjoy!"

Gabrielle sat next to Hope and as they

began to sing some of the choruses, she noticed that Hope sang with real feeling and didn't need to glance at the song sheet once. It was obviously a story that meant a lot to her. Gabrielle enjoyed getting to know the songs – some were heartbreaking, while others were catchy – and she began to fall in love with Angelica's character. She decided that "Family Now" was the best song of all…so she was thrilled when Angel Lara asked her to sing a solo section from it.

She cleared her throat and sang sweetly and clearly.

"Bravo, Gabrielle!" said the teacher when she finished. "You have such a pretty voice!"

Gabrielle blushed, but couldn't help beaming with delight.

Through the words of the songs,

Gabrielle began to work out the characters. There were the three sisters named Penelope, Peaches and Pandora Pomander, who befriended Angelica at the orphanage where they all lived. Penelope seemed a bit of a baby, while Pandora was a school prefect type. But Peaches was funny and cute, so that role interested Gabrielle. Deep down though, she knew that she really wanted to be Angelica.

I don't think I can compete with Hope, thought Gabrielle. *After all, she knows the songs already. But even if I don't stand much chance, I've got to at least try,* she decided. *I'm going to audition for it.* And she and the other girls merrily sang from their hearts all the way through music club.

* * *

Sunday passed in a blur of everyone talking about *Angelica*, and everywhere she went, Gabrielle heard girls humming, whistling and singing the songs from the show.

Soon it was Monday morning and time for lessons. The Cherubics were surprised when, after breakfast, Angel Fleur told them they were going to spend the morning in a baking class. Gabrielle and her three friends from Crystals chattered all the way to the gleaming Angel Academy kitchens, where Angel Honey, the cookery teacher, waited for them. Gabrielle gazed around at the dazzlingly white walls, the endless supply of stainless steel appliances and the shiny accessories hanging on overhead rails. There was every imaginable type of bowl, pot, pan and utensil. The room was divided into mini kitchens, each designed for two Cherubics to work at, with a white china sink, a double-oven, and various pastel-coloured store cupboards and matching range of kitchenware. Perhaps best of all though was the sweet smell in the air of freshly-baked sponge cakes.

Gabrielle turned to Ruth. "Maybe Angel Honey has been trying out today's recipe already!" she suggested.

"Mmmm, I think so too. Smells yummy," Ruth said. "But I'd much rather start rehearsals for the show than bake cakes!"

"I know *Angelica's* really thrilling," agreed Gabrielle. "But baking is fun too."

Gabrielle and Ruth made a beeline for the first workstation, which was themed with duck-egg blue equipment.

"Girls, before you get settled, come down to the front and watch my demonstration," Angel Honey called.

Angel Honey was a popular teacher, who always left a fragrant, blossom honey aroma behind her. "Let me tell you why you're here today," said Angel Honey. "We're going to practise making cupcakes, because you'll be baking them to serve to your parents when they come to see your show at the end of term. We want these cakes to be perfect and we don't have many lessons in which to practise, so do please concentrate."

The girls watched as the teacher demonstrated how to weigh, measure, and then mix the cupcake ingredients until the batter was as light and fluffy as possible, but Gabrielle noticed that Ruth was quietly humming songs during the demonstration – which sounded as if they were from the *Angelica* musical again. Other girls whispered and giggled and Gabrielle heard odd words like "Angelica", "costumes", "make-up" and "auditions". Nobody concentrated as well as they usually did in class and Gabrielle felt a little sorry for Angel Honey. Normally baking cupcakes would have been a very popular lesson indeed.

"Cherubics, what a noise," said Angel Honey. "Someone is singing. And lots of people are chattering. I trust you are all watching what I'm doing!"

She carried on with her demonstration, spooning little pools of creamed mixture into cupcake cases, then popping them into the hot oven.

"Right, over to you now!" said Angel Honey, after she'd iced a batch of previously baked and cooled cakes with pretty pastel colours.

The Cherubics all returned to their workstations and, after washing her hands, Gabrielle began to measure out the ingredients on the scales provided. But when she looked over at Ruth, her friend didn't seem to be measuring the quantities at all.

"Aren't you weighing anything?" asked Gabrielle.

"There's no need," said Ruth. "I watched what Angel Honey did. It looked easy. I'm *approximating* – it's one of my skills."

Gabrielle smiled. She remembered Mum giving her tips in their cosy kitchen at home, with its bright red stove and familiar wooden table; always stressing how important it was to measure things out exactly and follow the recipe. So many times they had whisked and chatted together, producing lovely cakes, buns and biscuits. And all the help and love Mum had given her, Gabrielle was going to put to good use at Angel Academy.

As Ruth combined her ingredients she began to hum the tune of one of the *Angelica* songs once more. Then she added the words. "*Buns with honey, taste so yummy, mmmm, honey buns…*" At first she whispered the words but then she sang a little louder and some of the other girls, who also knew the song, began to join in with the harmony. Gabrielle couldn't believe her ears as most of the Cherubics began to sing softly as they went about their baking tasks.

"I *can* hear you, you know!" Angel Honey said, with an indulgent smile. "I know you're all excited about the show, but you need to concentrate on your cupcakes now. Just keep the noise down a little…"

There was a ripple of laughter before the girls quietened down. But they were all still simmering, bubbling and brimming with excitement as they worked.

After placing their cake trays in the oven, they cleaned up the mess they'd made in their little kitchens, while the cakes turned golden.

When it was time to take them out, Ruth was not happy… "Oh no!" she shrieked.

"What's happened? I've only got one big cake, a horrible blob of a thing!"

Gabrielle stared. All Ruth's mixture had run together and formed one lump of cake, which had baked that way – and had not risen at all.

"Erm, poor you. Sometimes mixtures just don't quite work out," said Gabrielle sympathetically.

Ruth stared at Gabrielle's cakes. "Oh look! Your cakes are totally perfect. Just like Angel Honey's! It's not fair. I'm rubbish at this!" exclaimed Ruth. "Just like with sewing. My fingers are not made for creating stuff!"

Angel Honey came to look. "Ruth Bell, what happened here? Did you follow the recipe?"

Ruth shook her head, looking rather sheepish.

"Well, I do hope there's an improvement in your cakes before the end of term!" Angel Honey said firmly. "And it might be helpful if you could remember that you come to my class to bake, not to sing!"

"Yes, of course," said Ruth, her freckly cheeks blushing bright red. "I'm very sorry, Angel Honey! I got a bit carried away!"

While the cakes cooled, the girls polished all their utensils until they shone, replacing them carefully where they had found them. Then it was time for the icing. Ruth looked a little lost as everyone began to spread the creamy frosting over the top of their cakes.

"Why don't you ice a couple of mine?" suggested Gabrielle kindly.

"Oh, could I? Thanks so much," said Ruth.
Angel Honey had prepared some sugar
petals for them to finish off the cakes with.

"Nearly as good as Sparkles!" said
Gabrielle proudly as she formed pretty
flowers on the top of her cupcakes.

The girls were allowed to take their
cakes back to the dorm so they
carefully placed them in boxes before
setting off.

"Well, that was great fun," declared Hope,
as they fluttered back to Crystals.

"I know, I loved it," agreed Gabrielle.

"I didn't," said Ruth crossly. "I'm jinxed
at crafty things!"

"Cheer up," said Gabrielle. "Just
remember, we've always got *Angelica* to
look forward to!"

"Yes, I can't wait for the auditions," agreed Ruth. "Do you think we have time to go and see our chevalanges before lunch? It would be nice to tell them about the show."

"Oh yes, definitely. I'd love to see Domino," said Gabrielle. "Let's go to the stables."

Chapter 4

The fabulous winged horses known as chevalanges were stabled in the grounds of Angel Academy. Gabrielle visited her horse, Domino, whenever she felt in need of support and advice, but she also liked to see him at other times too. They'd had an extra-special relationship ever since he flew all the way to earth to collect Gabrielle for her first day at Angel Academy, and so she loved to take care of him and pamper him as much as possible whenever she had free time. The chevalanges were out grazing and lazing in the paddock and Gabrielle thought just how splendid Domino looked. Of course, all of the chevalanges were incredibly beautiful, but there was something extra majestic about Domino, with his shimmering, faintly dappled silver coat, and his finely contoured head with those magnificently thoughtful eyes, like pools of liquid chocolate.

"Hi, Domino!" cried Gabrielle. "You look very relaxed!"

"Gabrielle, how lovely to see you. I *am* relaxed. Are you looking forward to starting work on your Messenger Charm?" asked Domino.

"Yes, I can't wait – we've got our first lesson on it tomorrow," said Gabrielle. "But there's something else to tell you!"

"Really? What news do you have?" he asked.

"There's going to be a school production – and it's *Angelica* and the auditions are on Friday!" she said.

"That's great news. And it's a lovely story. I can see you're excited!" said Domino.

"Well, excited and a bit nervous," Gabrielle admitted.

"Ah," said Domino. "What's making you nervous?"

"Well, I so badly want to be in the show, but I also want to do well with the Messenger Charm, and I have baking and other stuff too!" Gabrielle explained, worries suddenly bubbling up inside her. "There's such a lot to do. And I'd never heard of the story of Angelica before so, while all the others know the songs, I'm having to start from scratch and, oh, I'd just love to be Angelica…" She paused to take a breath.

"Gabrielle, my advice to you is to take one thing at a time," said Domino. "Concentrate on the charm in lesson time and prepare for the show in rehearsals and in your free time."

"That's a good idea," said Gabrielle, nodding. "I must stop thinking of everything all at once!"

"There is a lot of pressure on you to learn fast because you've had less angel experiences than everyone else, but you are doing so well. Try to enjoy it all!" said Domino.

"I do!" said Gabrielle. "You know I love it here."

"Yes, I know," said Domino. "And what about going to the library to find a copy of *Angelica*? I'm sure that's what you would have done at home. Take the book out and lose yourself in the story. It's beautiful and I know you'd be wonderful as Angelica. In many ways you are very like her – kind and resourceful and loyal to your friends…"

"Oh, Domino, thank you. You always have such good ideas and you make me feel so much better about myself. I'll go and find the story straight after lunch."

*   *   *

After rushing her lunch, Gabrielle excused herself from her friends and went to the school library.

The librarian, Angel Sophie, greeted her with a warm smile.

"Do you have any copies of the story of *Angelica*?" Gabrielle asked shyly.

"Yes, I've looked out three copies," said Angel Sophie. "I thought they might be in demand before Madame Seraph distributes the full scripts. But you are the first to ask!"

She took Gabrielle to the shelf where they were.

"Thank you so much," said Gabrielle, and although she only had a short time before afternoon classes, she curled up on a padded window seat in a corner of the library and was transported into the world of the little orphaned angel. *How terrible for Angelica*, she thought, as she read about the tiny angel's lonely life, searching for food and shelter as the snow fell all around. *I can't imagine what life would be like without my mother or father. They're always there if I need them, even if I don't see them every day now.*

The story made her realize how hard it must have been for her mum, who had had to grow up without her own mother. Gabrielle's granny had been a full angel who was unable to stay with her human husband and daughter because she couldn't survive on earth. *Poor Mum!*

Time flew by and when the librarian

tapped her shoulder, Gabrielle suddenly realized that it was time for class.

"Sorry!" said Gabrielle. "I was lost in another world. I'm enjoying the story so much – but it's making me feel sad too."

The librarian nodded. "That's what good stories do. Make you feel as if it's happening to you."

It was all Gabrielle could think of during afternoon classes. At bedtime that night, she undressed quickly, put on her nightdress, brushed her teeth, combed her hair and placed her halo on the silver halo stand by her bed. Then she climbed hastily under her pale blue quilt, and couldn't resist taking the book out again.

"What's that you've got there, Gabrielle?" asked Ruth.

"Erm, I just borrowed the *Angelica* story from the library, because I don't really know it," she explained.

"Oh, that's a good idea. I think you should audition for the part of Angelica, Gabrielle, because you are a lovely singer," whispered Ruth. "You did so well at music club."

"Do you think so?" asked Gabrielle, daring to admit to herself just how much she wanted the role. "Do you really think I have a chance?"

"Yes, of course," said Ruth. "A good chance. I'm thinking of going for one of the Pomander sisters – they have more fun!"

Gabrielle devoured every word of the story. About how the adorable little Angelica was found by the Snow Angel and taken to the orphanage, where an angel called Mercy took charge of her care.

Gabrielle felt salty tears trickle down her cheeks as she thought about Angelica, with no parents of her own. It made her think about Mum and Dad again and all the lovely times at home she'd had as a little girl, and how much fun she had with them in the school holidays. She couldn't stop rereading the story, but soon it was time for lights out, so she reluctantly put the book down.

Gabrielle was soon fast asleep but her dreams were full of Angelica, cold and all alone in the snow.

Chapter 5

The next morning, the Cherubics had a double lesson of games out on the lawns. While they played feather ball, where they had to use a racquet to hit a very light ball across a net, all the chatter was about the school production. Gabrielle and Hope had teamed up and were playing doubles against Fey and Merry.

"I'm going to do everything in my power

to be Angelica," said Hope between shots.

Gabrielle smiled. "You would definitely be great as her," she said.

"Do you think so?" said Hope. "But there are such a lot of lines to learn for that role, so I don't know if I can do it. Charity's much better at memorizing things than me, but it's not as if I could get Charity to learn the lines for me, is it?"

"Erm, I suppose not, because you're the one who would have to say them!" laughed Gabrielle.

The twins were complete opposites; while Charity loved to read books and study, Hope preferred to do lively things and have fun.

"Do you think lots of people will want to try for the part?" asked Gabrielle.

"Yes, definitely, loads will. Merry really wants it too. What about you?"

"Yes, I'd love to. But I feel a bit behind everyone else because I'd never even heard of the story before," said Gabrielle. "Never mind the songs."

Hope shrugged. "We'll just have to try our best at the auditions. Do you want to practise some of the songs together? I have no trouble with the songs. I've known them nearly all my life."

"That would be great," said Gabrielle. "Thanks so much."

When Gabrielle and Hope got back to Crystals at the end of games, they found Ruth and Charity poring over a copy of all the parts for the auditions on Friday.

"Ooooh, it's arrived! Please let me see," said Gabrielle.

Her eyes scanned it urgently.

Angelica – the heroine

Penelope Pomander – an orphan

Peaches Pomander – Penelope's little sister

Pandora Pomander – the eldest Pomander sister

Mercy – runs the orphanage

Diana – Angelica's mother

Dominic – Angelica's father

Millie – Angelica's friend

Fern – another orphan

Tatiana – a helper at the orphanage

Other angels at the orphanage

There was a section of script to learn for each character you wanted to try out for, as well as copies of all the songs.

"Let's help each other by saying the other lines for one another as we practise," suggested Gabrielle.

"That's a great idea," said Ruth.

"I'll just help everyone," said Charity kindly. "I'm not auditioning for any roles. I'd love to direct the show instead. I've got all these ideas about how it should look, and how all the lines should be said, and when the music should come in. Maybe I'll be allowed to do something like that."

"They'll be mad if they don't let you help at least," said Gabrielle. "You'd be brilliant, because you're so organized and systematic about everything."

"Thanks, Gabrielle!" said Charity. "Anyway, come on, everyone, it's time for our next class!"

* * *

The girls were all very busy thinking about the show, but they were equally excited about the new charm they were due to start working on. And after a lovely lunch of soup and apple sponge pudding, it was finally time to find out more about it. Gabrielle was full of curiosity as she floated to her first Messenger Charm lesson.

The Cherubics were surprised to see some other, older angels in the classroom, sitting in a semicircle around the teacher. They weren't pupils at Angel Academy, but didn't look that much older than final year students.

I wonder why they're here? thought Gabrielle, and she could tell that the other Cherubics were thinking the same.

Everyone shrugged their shoulders.

Ruth put her hand up but before she had the chance to ask about it, Angel Leonora, the Messenger Charm teacher, addressed the girls.

"Welcome, everyone. As you will have noticed, I have a little surprise for you," said the teacher. "This afternoon I have invited along some fully trained Guardian Angels who are going to answer any questions you may have about messages and when they are used during Guardian Angel missions. These are former pupils of Angel Academy who have been through the training you are doing now and have gone on to fulfil their potential as full Guardian Angels. Let's welcome them warmly."

The Cherubics applauded enthusiastically.

"Just think, we're going to be that cool one day," said Ruth.

"I hope so!" said Gabrielle, who could hardly imagine what it would be like to be a full Guardian Angel instead of a Cherubic at Angel Academy – it seemed such a long way off.

"I will begin by explaining just how important it is to retrieve and remember messages during Guardian Angel duties," said Angel Leonora. She looked around to check that she had her students' full attention before continuing. "The fact is that our messages can save human lives. When you go to earth, there will be times when you need to be guided on your mission. It might be that you need to know a location or a development in a dangerous situation. For example, there was one mission, many moons ago, when a human was being encircled by a rapidly spreading forest fire. We sent a message to a Guardian Angel, and because she recalled the location from the message perfectly, she

 was able to lead the human out of danger."

Wow, that's incredible, thought Gabrielle, as she began to realize what a difference they would be able to make to humans once fully trained.

"It's important to know why we train you as we do," said Angel Leonora. "Everything we teach you has a purpose for your future lives as Guardian Angels. Now, any questions?"

Merry had one. "Why do we have to stay a secret to humans? What harm would it do if they saw us?" she quizzed.

An angel called Emerald leaned forward to answer. She had dark hair, with china-doll pale skin and rosebud red lips.

Gabrielle, as the only Earth Angel at the school, was especially interested in the answer to this question.

"We do not want angels and humans to mix too much, because the more they know about our healing and caring ways, the less powerful we may be for them," she said. "Secrecy is the key to our powers. And, when angels and humans fall in love, for example, it can be complicated. Angels cannot live permanently on earth, so relationships can be tricky."

Gabrielle knew this only too well. Her angel grandmother had fallen in love with Gabrielle's human grandpa during an earth mission, but because she could not survive on earth as a full angel, she'd had to leave her baby and husband behind and return to the angel world, where she died of a broken heart. It always made Gabrielle sad to think of it, as her mum had missed out on knowing her mother, and Grandpa was heartbroken to this day at losing his young wife.

Gabrielle tried not to dwell on these sad thoughts. Luckily she was distracted as Ruth's hand shot up with the next question.

"How are the messages delivered?" she asked.

A beautiful Guardian Angel called Tulle

raised a hand to indicate she would answer the question.

"You will be drawn towards an object, such as a feather or leaf, and when you say a spell over it, the object will float before you and a message will appear," she replied. "Then, when you've memorized the words, you must remember to make the message invisible again using another spell."

Charity wanted to know the spell.

Tulle explained. "It's:

'*Angel bright, Angel sight,*
Show the note, Make it float.'

And when you have memorized it, you say: '*Message clear, Have no fear.*'"

Gabrielle thought that sounded like a wonderful system and it made her tingle to think that she had probably seen objects on earth which, unknown to her, had contained secret angel messages. She raised her hand this time.

"What sorts of messages might you leave for one another?" she asked curiously.

Another of the angels, called Iris, took up this question.

"Good question," she began. "The messages are very brief, such as *Meet the chevalanges at Featherwing Woods. Or Protect humans from avalanche, lead them to shelter at Snowy Gorge.*"

"Wow, this sounds exciting!" whispered Ruth. "I can't wait to make a difference to people's lives."

Gabrielle smiled in agreement. *How brilliant*, she thought. Angels think of everything. No wonder humans could never detect them on earth – it was all thanks to invisibility powers, which they had learned about in the last charm, and now secret messages.

It was time for the older angels to leave and they called "goodbye" and "good luck" to the young Cherubics as they went. The rest of the lesson was spent memorizing the spells and also messages of no more than fifteen words, which Angel Leonora said was the ideal length – long enough to be useful but short enough to be easily remembered. She also emphasized the importance of reading the message carefully and recalling every word exactly as it had appeared.

"This will be easy," said Gabrielle. "Fifteen words? I can remember whole songs and poems."

But it was harder than Gabrielle had imagined. She found she could recall the meaning of a phrase, but not the precise words.

"You might want to try turning the messages into chants," suggested the teacher. "That sometimes helps."

First, Ruth gave one to Gabrielle:

"Fly to the nightingale tree and wait for the sound of a cuckoo."

Gabrielle tried to recall it as best she could...

"Fly to the cuckoo tree and wait for the sound of a nightingale," she said confidently.

"Nope!" laughed Ruth as she checked the message.

"Seriously?" said Gabrielle, trying to think again. "Are you kidding around?

I'm sure it was a cuckoo and a nightingale."

"Try again," said Ruth.

"Fly to the nightingale tree and wait for the cuckoo?"

"Still nope!" said Ruth.

"Wow, this is really hard. Who knew that remembering fewer than fifteen words would be so impossible?"

Gabrielle then turned it into a chant as the teacher had suggested.

"Fly to the nightingale tree
And wait for the sound
Of a cuckoo!" she chanted.

She and Ruth sang messages back and forth to one another and eventually got the hang of retaining every word. After that, they swapped partners with Hope and Charity, and Gabrielle gave a message to Hope.

It read: *An avalanche is gathering, take shelter by the big fir tree.*

Hope's first attempt was: "There's been an avalanche so stay by the fir tree…" Then she said: "People are gathering fir trees, so beware of the avalanche…"

And so it went on, until Gabrielle had to show her the message because she couldn't get it at all.

"This is hard work!" Hope complained.

Gabrielle nodded sympathetically.

"Charity is much better at stuff like this!" said Hope.

"It'll get easier," said Gabrielle. She thought about the way that it always seemed an impossible dream to earn a charm when you first started learning about it. But she knew from past experience that you did eventually get the knack of it. Gabrielle began to wonder if Charity was having similar thoughts, because she raised her hand and asked:

"Excuse me, Angel Leonora. What will happen on the day of the charm test?"

"That's a very good question. The test for the Messenger Charm is about homing in on messages, remembering them and acting on them," explained their teacher. "Most of all, it's a test of memory." She paused for a moment, and then, as if she thought she had perhaps made it all sound much too simple, she went on, "Do remember – if we get one tiny bit of a message wrong when we are out and about on full Guardian Angel duties, then we might fail to help the human in distress in the best way possible.

That would be a very serious situation and could have terrible consequences," she finished solemnly.

Gabrielle left the lesson with a great sense of the significance of being a Guardian Angel. She only hoped she'd be able to manage it herself, like the impressive older girls they'd just met – who had once been Cherubics too.

Chapter 6

Much as the girls were excited about the
Messenger Charm, their thoughts turned
back to the school musical very quickly.
Gabrielle knew that she, Merry and Hope
all desperately wanted to be Angelica, while
Ruth seemed very keen to be Pandora. In
some moments, Gabrielle thought of not
auditioning for Angelica at all, rather than
go up for it against her friends. Then in

other moments, she thought she may as
well give it a try because maybe neither of
her friends would get it, and then she'd
always wonder if she might have been the
lucky one.

On Wednesday afternoon it was warm
and still, and the gardens of Angel
Academy were fragrant with scented
white jasmine. Birds chirped tunefully in
the trees and there was a gentle sound of
the waters of the lake lapping softly
on its shore. Madame Seraph sent
the messenger doves around to say
they'd all have a picnic tea that evening,
by the huge willow tree at the edge of
the lake.

"Wow, what's an angel picnic like?"
asked Gabrielle. "It sounds heavenly."

"They're super-delicious," said Ruth.

"I can imagine! Yum!" said Gabrielle.

After an extra singing lesson for anyone who wanted to audition for the show, it was time for tea. The Cherubics from Crystals flew down to the lakeside excitedly.

The school catering staff never let the girls down. The spread of food on the picnic tables was tremendous and Gabrielle realized she was famished. There were scrumptious sandwiches, salads and dips, fresh fruit kebabs with chocolate sauce, dainty butterfly cakes with vanilla butter icing, fresh cream angel meringues and squidgy, gooey marshmallows. There were jugs of cloudy lemonade and pretty pink glasses lining the tables too, as well as floral napkins and tiny posies of wild flowers.

The girls settled down on chairs at the
pretty rainbow-coloured picnic tables.
Gabrielle sat beside Merry and Hope, while
Ruth and Charity sat opposite and chatted
away about the personality of Pandora and
how she should be played. Charity still
wanted to direct the show and Gabrielle
thought she'd be perfect to do so.

"We've only got two days until the
auditions now," Gabrielle said to Merry and
Hope. "I almost know my lines but why don't
we help each other to get into character?"
she suggested.

"That sounds like a good idea," said Merry.

"Yes, I'm up for that," said Hope.

So Gabrielle, Hope and Merry devised
a plan of action where they would meet as
often as possible in the gardens over the next

two days, to sing songs from the musical and listen to each other saying the lines from the audition sheets for Angelica.

"Let's start straight after the picnic," said Gabrielle.

After eating so much that she felt she might burst, Gabrielle and her two friends flew over to a wooden bench near an avenue of trees where no one would disturb them.

"Why don't we listen to each other saying our audition speeches," suggested Merry. I'll go first if you like!"

Merry cleared her throat and then, without looking at her notes once, she began to recite the speech for Angelica. She was word-perfect. Gabrielle and Hope were surprised how well she knew it. So far, Gabrielle could only remember some sections of it, and Hope had not learned any lines at all.

"Wow! That's impressive," said Gabrielle, when Merry had finished. "Well done. You've inspired me to work harder on this."

"I'll be word-perfect for next time too!" declared Hope.

"It takes a bit of work to memorize the lines," said Merry.

"Yes and I will do the work," said Hope, a little sharply.

"I just can't believe how well you know the lines already, Merry," said Gabrielle. "You really deserve the part."

But Hope didn't say another word. Instead she flew off, leaving the other two looking at each other and wondering what they'd done wrong.

Next morning, it was time for another baking lesson. Gabrielle and Ruth went to the same workstation as before, while Merry and Hope were behind them, with Charity and Fey opposite.

Angel Honey began the lesson by congratulating everyone on the cupcakes they'd baked in the last lesson.

"Erm, in my case, she should just say 'cake' because I ended up with one giant one!" whispered Ruth.

Gabrielle giggled. "Today is going to be your lucky day!" she said.

"Yes, because my days of *approximation* are over!" said Ruth. "I'm going to measure everything this time!"

Angel Honey had another plate of delicious-looking goodies to reveal.

"Today, we're going to try butterfly cakes with butter icing, a variation on the classic cupcake," said Angel Honey.

"Oooh, yummy," said Gabrielle. "We had these at the picnic last night, didn't we?"

"Yes, I love them," said Ruth.

Gabrielle and Ruth decided to help each other weigh and measure their ingredients this time, working closely together after Ruth's previous disaster. But as they carefully tipped and poured, they were suddenly distracted by a squeal from Hope: "Oh, Merry! Be careful!"

Gabrielle looked round to see that Merry had turned the tap on full blast in their kitchen area and soaked Hope.

"Sorrreee!" said Merry. "It was an accident. I can't help it if the tap is super-powerful!"

Hope dried herself off with a towel and everyone got back to work. However, as Gabrielle was helping Ruth to weigh the butter accurately, she thought she saw a puff of flour out of the corner of her eye.

Gabrielle spun round and gasped as she saw Hope throwing a handful of flour at Merry.

Merry sneezed, which caught the attention of Angel Honey, who was helping one of the other bakers.

"That's enough, girls, settle down," the teacher called.

But as Angel Honey turned away, Merry flicked a handful of flour towards Hope. Hope immediately returned fire with a handful of her own, leaving Merry dusted with white. All the other girls stopped what they were doing to watch.

"Whatever's going on?" said Angel Honey, noticing the disturbance and floating back towards them with a frown on her face.

"She soaked me," said Hope.

"It was an accident," said Merry. "You threw the flour on purpose. That's different."

"Girls, I will not have this silly nonsense in my class!" said Angel Honey, very firmly indeed.

"Merry *did* soak her," piped up Larissa.

"But she didn't mean it," said Fey.

"Be quiet! Everyone!" said Angel Honey. "We've a lot to get through this morning."

For a little while, all of the Cherubics worked cheerfully together.

But then there was another commotion at Hope and Merry's workstation.

"What's going on now, girls?" asked Angel Honey crossly.

"Merry started it," said Hope. "She said I'd be lucky to get the part as I didn't know my lines."

"No, no, that's not true," said Merry indignantly. "I was just repeating what you'd said – that there are so many lines and you're not sure you can remember them all."

"It's because you want to be Angelica and you can't bear the thought of anyone else having the part, isn't it?" Hope said, her hands on her hips and looking very cross now.

"Girls, that's enough. You are *angels*; your role is to be kind to others – and that includes other angels. Now please get on with your baking," said Angel Honey.

Once again everyone returned to the task in hand and the rest of the lesson went smoothly, though it was clear that Merry and Hope weren't speaking to each other.

Gabrielle worried about her two friends as they mixed, stirred and baked without a single word or smile. It was so unusual to see them behaving like this.

The cakes turned out nicely – even Ruth's – and the girls cut out butterfly wings before decorating their cakes in sparkly pinks, purples and other gorgeous colour combinations.

As they were about to leave, Angel Honey stopped them and said, "Girls, the show is always a highlight of the year; it's meant to be enjoyable and fun. But, as I believe you have been told, it's not meant to get in the way of your work or your friendships. Please think about that."

"I'm so, so sorry," said Hope, looking tearful now. "I didn't want to quarrel with Merry. It was just a silly misunderstanding."

"Yes, we didn't mean it," said Merry. "I'm sorry too!"

Both girls looked very upset and the rest of the Cherubics looked over at them with sympathy.

"All right, girls. It's time for your next lesson. Off you go now."

As they were about to leave, Angel Fleur floated into the kitchen with some documents for Angel Honey. Gabrielle was at the back of the line and she was sure she could hear Angel Honey telling Angel Fleur about what had gone on between Merry and Hope.

The girls didn't have any time to discuss what had happened because they had to rush to their next lesson, but as they took their seats in the Ambroserie at lunchtime, Madame Seraph appeared before them and held up her hand for silence.

Oh no, thought Gabrielle, *Madame has never made an announcement on a Thursday before. What is she going to say?*

Chapter 7

A hush fell over the Ambroserie as the Cherubics all stopped what they were doing to listen to the Head Angel.

"Girls, I have a very important announcement to make," Madame Seraph said in her melodious voice. "It has been brought to my attention that there has been some disruptive behaviour going on in the school, with some of you arguing over who will get parts in the show. The show is supposed to encourage teamwork and harmony. I said last Saturday that if the show interfered with an angel's schoolwork in any way, we would have to take action. Well, I'm afraid at the moment I'm wondering if I should allow the show to go ahead…"

A collective gasp rippled across the Ambroserie. This was worse than expected, as far as Gabrielle was concerned.

"I know this would be very disappointing," said Madame Seraph, "and it's not a decision I make lightly. So you have twenty-four hours in which to redeem yourselves. There is lots to do to prepare for the show that requires you all to work together, and if I see many examples of cooperation as you work on these tasks and as you go about your normal classes, then the show will go ahead and the auditions will take place tomorrow afternoon in the theatre as planned. But if I am not impressed by your behaviour, then the show is most certainly OFF!" And with that, she vanished.

The girls were very quiet as they floated off for their afternoon lessons, stunned by Madame's announcement.

Gabrielle heard a few mumbles of "This is all Hope and Merry's fault!" and, "A flour fight…so not like angels!"

It was too awful to think of the show being cancelled before the auditions had even begun, but Gabrielle didn't want to blame her friends. The girls arrived in the art department, where they were supposed to be designing posters for *Angelica*. There were still mutterings and moans about the flour fight and Gabrielle could see that wasn't going to get them anywhere. So when the art teacher, Angel Bellissima, went away to collect some poster paints, Gabrielle decided to speak up.

"Listen, everyone," she said. "If we start to argue about who is to blame, Madame will never allow the show to go ahead. We *have* to get along – that's what Madame Seraph expects of us. She said so at lunch, didn't she? Let's try really hard to work together. It's our only hope."

"You're right," said Ruth.

The other Cherubics all agreed.

Gabrielle could hardly bear to think

about what it would be like if Madame did not allow the show to go on. They *had* to pull together.

The next day was Friday – and the day of the *Angelica* auditions, if Madame Seraph allowed them to go ahead. Gabrielle woke very early with a feeling of excitement and anxiety in her tummy. She was looking forward to trying out for the roles so much – but like all the other Cherubics, she had no idea what Madame Seraph would decide.

She went to the bathroom to wash. When she was finished, she looked into the mirror and began to sing some of the lines from Angelica's main song.

"*It's snowing in my heart.*
It's freezing in my head.

Heat my heart, warm my head.
Tuck me into a cosy bed…"

After that, she ran through the lines for the two parts she'd be auditioning for. That of Angelica, of course:

"Oh, Mercy, you've been like a mother to me, but if there is any chance my real mother is alive then I'd like to find her… I hope you can understand?"

And for Peaches: "Life in the orphanage was no fun until you arrived, Angelica. What will we do without you? Please don't leave…in fact…can I come with you? Pleeease don't leave me here!"

With the competition so fierce for the part of Angelica, Gabrielle had decided it would be a good idea to have a back-up plan – and she really did love the character of

Peaches. And so, with her two speeches memorized, she felt ready for the auditions – if only they would take place.

Throughout the morning, Gabrielle and the other Cherubics worked together helping Angel Willow the sewing teacher make alterations to costumes for the

show, which gave them hope that it wasn't cancelled just yet. The Cherubics did everything they could to cooperate with each other. In fact they were super-helpful – even Ruth, who hated sewing, did her bit, stitching without complaint.

Surely Madame Seraph will let the show go on now! thought Gabrielle.

The morning seemed to stretch out for ever. At lunch, the Cherubics were all very quiet and subdued, as they still didn't know what Madame's decision would be. Even though a delicious pasta bake with a crunchy cheese topping was served with a salad bathed in honey and lemon, and dessert was a fruity banana split, the Cherubics did no more than push the food around their plates, as they anxiously waited for news about *Angelica*.

"Here comes Madame Seraph!" cried Hope, as she spotted the Head Angel out of the corner of her eye.

Gabrielle could feel the tension in the Ambroserie as they awaited the announcement, she and the others trying not to read too much into the expression on Madame's face.

Madame whispered to Angel Fleur, then to Angel Lara, and also to Angel Willow. It was impossible to work out what she was saying. At last, she appeared in her usual place in the middle of the floor.

"I have given the show a great deal of thought this morning," the Head Angel began. "I've taken advice from staff who have observed the Cherubics in their various classes. There has been a lot of information about behaviour, manners and attitudes… And I am pleased to say that everyone has cooperated very nicely together. Therefore, I have decided that the show will go ahead. Auditions will proceed this afternoon as planned and a list of times

will be posted on the theatre door.
Cherubics, you should proceed to the
theatre after lunch. Good luck to all!"

"Hurrah!" As cheers went up all round
the dining room, Hope and Merry broke
into huge smiles and hugged each other.

Chapter 8

Angels Lara and Fleur were in charge of the auditions for *Angelica*, which were to take place on the school stage itself. It was a deep stage, with wings to either side, a polished wooden floor and bright spotlights along the front. Gabrielle had never been on it before.

The girls from Crystals arrived at the theatre door together and read the notice pinned there:

Decisions made by Angel Lara and Angel Fleur will be final. It is important that we are pleased and proud for those who get the main parts, but all contributors to the success of the show are equally important.

Gabrielle looked down the list and saw that she was due to audition just after Hope.

"You should sit in the audience seats while waiting to be called," Angel Fleur told them.

"That means we'll all be able to see each other audition, making it even more scary!" said Gabrielle, as they chose seats near the front.

"Yes, I know," said Ruth. "But if you're shy, there's not much point auditioning for a show!"

"True," agreed Gabrielle, with a smile.

They all sat nervously in the auditorium. Merry was next to Gabrielle and squeezed her hand.

"It's only a show!" she said. "Don't worry too much."

Gabrielle nodded, trying her best to relax.

Merry was one of the first Cherubics to go up onstage. Gabrielle noticed how clear and crisp Merry's voice was as she spoke her lines with passion and sincerity. As for her singing – it was as sweet as a nightingale's.

"Great singing!" said Gabrielle, as Merry came back to her seat. "You were fab!"

"Really? Thanks," said Merry. "It was all a bit of a blur."

Then Hope's name was called.

"Good luck!" said Gabrielle.

"Yes, all the best!" said Merry.

"Thanks," said Hope. "I'm looking forward to this."

Gabrielle began to panic, realizing she was next. *I don't know the lines for either part!* she thought.

I don't know the words to the songs, she then decided.

I'm no good at musicals.

I don't look right for the part of Angelica.

I should want this part for my friends as they want it so badly. Oh dear, why am I competing with them?

As Hope began her audition, Gabrielle froze. The spotlights shone on Hope, and she looked lovely: dainty and vulnerable, just as Gabrielle imagined Angelica. Hope was *brilliant*. She was word-perfect; she sang the songs beautifully, and she danced well too, performing lovely spins. Gabrielle was a bit surprised at just how good Hope was. She'd obviously worked really hard on her lines since Wednesday, when she'd known none of them. *I knew it wasn't a good idea to watch each other*, she thought. *I can never be as good as Hope.*

Hope came bounding back to her seat after her audition.

"How did I sound?" she asked anxiously. "I sang for my life! All the words just came to me. I can't believe it! It was such good fun."

"You were completely awesome!" said Gabrielle. "I just hope I can do the same."

"Good luck," said Hope. "I'm sure you'll be amazing."

"Yes, good luck!" said Merry.

Gabrielle's throat felt very dry and tight as she walked through the wings. The stage seemed so big and wide now she was the only one on it. She floated over to the spotlight, which shone in the middle, marking where she had to stand. When she looked out to the seating area, it was quite dark, although she could make out Angel Fleur and Angel Lara, who were the nicest and most supportive angels you could imagine, as well as her friends sitting in the front rows. *Everyone is on my side,* Gabrielle told herself; *they are my friends. So there is really nothing to worry about – nothing at all.*

But despite telling herself this, over and over again, she felt quite overwhelmed. Isolated. Her head began to spin.

She could hardly swallow. All she wanted was to go back to Crystals and sing the songs into the bathroom mirror. She didn't want to be here right now, putting herself on the line.

"Ah, hello, Gabrielle," said Angel Lara. "Please sing Angelica's song first, then say her section of script. Then finally, dance. Whenever you're ready…"

Gabrielle nodded, not trusting words to come out of her parched mouth.

One of the older angels struck up on the piano and, after the introductory bars, Gabrielle prepared to launch into the words she knew so well. She had run through them in her head a thousand times.

She began to sing:

"Oh, how I wish I had a mum and a dad…

Not having parents is making me sad…"

But the words were not hitting the air; they were wobbling almost silently on her lips and falling away to the ground.

Gabrielle saw Angel Fleur bring up one hand to stop the pianist. "We can't quite hear you, Gabrielle!" she said. "Would you like to start again?"

"Yes, please," whispered Gabrielle, with a nod.

She started again, softly and tremulously. The words floated in the air this time, rather than falling away. Gabrielle wanted to get the part of Angelica so much that she ached for it, and now she tried to forget everyone watching her and she *became*

Angelica. In fact, she got so caught up in Angelica's tragic story that she actually began to sob as she got to the end of the song.

"Oh, I'm sorry!" she gasped. "It's so sad. I just can't help it."

"Don't worry, dear Gabrielle," said Angel Fleur. "It's understandable. Now deliver the section of script if you can, please, followed by the dance."

"Yes, of course," said Gabrielle. The rest of her audition for the part of Angelica passed in a blur.

Because she also wanted to audition for the part of Peaches, Gabrielle had to remain onstage and go through the same procedure again, but with different words. It felt like torture, but she made it through to the end.

"Thank you, Gabrielle. Please go back to your seat," said Angel Fleur. It was impossible to know from her tone what she thought of Gabrielle's performance.

Gabrielle flew to the theatre seating area, where her friends were waiting.

"Don't worry about crying," said Ruth, giving her a hug. "You looked so sweet up there. Like you really *were* Angelica. It was very emotional!"

"But I totally messed up Angelica's song," said Gabrielle.

"You really didn't," said Hope. "You were lovely as her."

"I could have done it much better," said Gabrielle sadly.

"Chin up, Gabrielle," said Ruth. "Apparently we're not going to find out who has which parts until Monday, so there's no point in worrying about it just now. Let's enjoy the weekend."

Gabrielle felt very deflated. *How could I have messed up so badly?* she thought. And now there was a whole weekend to wait before finding out if she had got a part at all.

Chapter 9

Gabrielle did her best to put the audition out of her mind. Luckily, the weekend passed quickly in a whirl of picnics and games in the spring sunshine, set to the sound of the music club. The Cherubics who didn't want to act and some of the older girls had formed an orchestra and they could be heard practising the songs for the show with gusto.

* * *

When Gabrielle woke up on Monday
morning, she knew she'd have to face the
decisions about parts for the show.
However, first it was time for another
Messenger Charm lesson and Gabrielle
knew she had to concentrate on that.

The girls were told to meet
Angel Leonora in one of
the meadows near the
paddocks after breakfast.
It was a perfect spring
morning; the sky was china-blue
and cloudless, while a tapestry of red,
yellow and iris-blue wild flowers grew in
lovely tangles amongst the long grasses.

Angel Leonora was ready to begin.
"Today, Cherubics," she said, "the objective

for each of you is to locate a message in a natural object using the angel dust in your halos. You may not be aware that this dust acts as a homing device for you when you are on Guardian Angel missions. If you allow the angel dust to work its magic, you will find yourself being drawn in a particular direction. Then, once you have found the object that your halo has led you to, you should say the words: '*Angel bright, Angel sight, Show the note, Make it float*'.

"At this point the object will float up, and the message will appear to you in sparkly letters in the air. It's very important that you take enough time to memorize it, then say the words: '*Message clear, Have no fear.*'"

"I had no idea that halos could do that!"

Gabrielle whispered to Ruth. "This is going to be great fun."

She couldn't wait to see how it felt when her halo drew her towards a particular location.

"I had kind of forgotten about it," said Ruth. "My mum told me once. But until you start doing the training and dealing with messages, the angel dust doesn't do anything!"

Angel Leonora carried on with the instructions. "You will each have a unique message to learn, then you will repeat it to me in order to prove you've memorized it. Take your time. It's not a race. My assistant, Angel Charlie, will set you all off at slightly different times and I will wait for you by the lake. Are there any questions?"

The girls formed a queue.

"I can't wait for this!" said Gabrielle.
But despite her enthusiasm, she somehow
ended up at the back of the line. It felt like
an age until it was her turn to go and she
watched as each of her friends headed off in
search of a message. *I wonder how it will feel
to be controlled by angel dust,* she thought.
It was funny to see the other Cherubics as
they were propelled in certain directions by
the pull of their halo. At first they looked
like puppets being pulled by invisible
strings, but as they got used to letting the
angel dust work its magic, they began to fly
smoothly once more. It looked like there
were messages everywhere –
under toadstools and stones,
in leaves, feathers and flowers.

At last Gabrielle was next to go and on the say-so of Angel Charlie, off she went.

Gabrielle felt an extraordinary sensation which she'd never experienced before. It was as if she had no control over where she was heading, and at first she fought against the way her halo seemed to be pulling her, in a bid to stay in control. Then she realized she should relax and allow the halo to guide her if she wanted to find out where her message was.

She flew for a while before noticing that her halo was pulling her towards the middle of a bunch of daffodils. As she hovered over the cluster of pretty spring flowers, she said the spell.

"Angel bright, Angel sight, Show the note, Make it float."

Before her eyes, sparkly words projected
in the air as a message appeared. *Meet me
at the tulips to tell me what you know!* it read.
Gabrielle recited the message to herself a
few times, then, once she was sure of it,
she said the rest of the spell: "*Message clear,
Never fear.*" The message vanished.

She headed off in the direction of the
patch of fiery orange and yellow tulips that
she knew were in full bloom near the lake,
hoping that was where Angel Leonora
would be. She flew at top speed, chanting
the message over and over in her mind so as
not to forget it.

As she approached the tulip patch,
she could see that Angel Leonora and the
other Cherubics were indeed waiting there
for her. Gabrielle landed and whispered

the message to the teacher.

"Well done, Gabrielle," said Angel Leonora. "That was perfect."

As Gabrielle looked round for her friends so they could head back up to school together, she noticed Ruth and Charity huddled round Hope, who seemed to be upset.

Gabrielle flew over as fast as she could. "What's the matter?" she asked.

"Hope's a bit sad that she couldn't remember the message," said Charity, smoothing her sister's soft brown hair.

"Oh, you poor thing," said Gabrielle.

"I couldn't recall the message at all," sobbed Hope. "I thought I'd remembered it, but the words just wouldn't come. I'm the only one who messed up!"

"Never mind," said Gabrielle. "It's why we

have to practise. You'll be good at it soon, just you wait and see."

"But what if I don't pass the Messenger Charm test?" asked Hope with a tremor in her voice.

Gabrielle and Ruth shared a concerned glance. No one had failed to earn a charm. Yet!

Chapter 10

Even though the Messenger Charm lesson
had been fun and full of surprises, Gabrielle
was still longing to hear who'd got the main
parts for the show.

Later that day, a buzz went round Angel
Academy that Madame Seraph was about
to send out the list of names and parts for
Angelica via the messenger doves. During
afternoon break, the girls gathered in their

dorms. Gabrielle and her friends were so impatient to hear the news that they couldn't decide what to do. But all of a sudden, Sylvie took off from her perch on the windowsill, which was always a clear signal that she was going to pick up a message for them.

"Not long to wait now!" said Ruth.

"Oh, this suspense is dreadful!" said Gabrielle. "I want to know who is who... and yet I don't want to know."

"Same," agreed Ruth. "I so hope you're Angelica because you looked perfect onstage during the audition."

"There's no way it will be me," said Gabrielle. "I messed up and couldn't even sing the song loudly enough."

"Don't say that!" said Ruth. "It'll be fine

once the decisions are out of the way, you'll see."

Hope was unusually anxious as she waited to find out if she'd been picked as the orphaned angel. She went to peer out of the open window.

"Sylvie's coming back now!" she shrieked.

The Cherubics danced restlessly around Crystals until Sylvie arrived. "I have the cast list!" she announced, unrolling it expertly with her beak and wings.

The girls all gathered round the little bird excitedly.

Sylvie began: "Angelica will be played by…Hope Honeychurch!"

Hope leaped around ecstatically. "Yes, yes, it's me! Woo-hoo!"

Gabrielle tried to look pleased for Hope. But, even though she'd known all along that her audition hadn't gone well, she was bitterly disappointed that she hadn't got the part.

"Perhaps it's for the best," said Ruth, giving Gabrielle a gentle hug.

"I'm fine with it," said Gabrielle. "I would have got upset every time I played Angelica if I'd got the part, because I hate thinking of her all alone."

Sylvie waited patiently until she had the girls' attention once more. "Peaches Pomander will be played by Gabrielle Divine – how lovely! ...Pandora Pomander will be played by Ruth Bell – that's what you wanted, Ruth!

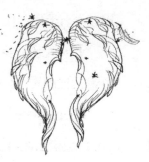

…And the show will be directed by Angel Fleur, with the help of Charity Honeychurch. Hurrah – a very fitting director!"

The girls didn't listen to the rest of the cast list. Three of them were delighted with the outcome, while Gabrielle quickly managed to accept the news properly. She loved the part of Peaches and, after getting so upset in the audition for Angelica, it was little wonder she hadn't got the main role. Her first thought now was to congratulate her friends.

"Well done, everyone!" said Gabrielle, hugging Ruth, then Hope, then Charity.

"I can't believe it!" Hope kept saying. "I'm never picked for anything. It's just unbelievable! I knew I'd done well, but I still can't take it in."

"You auditioned brilliantly, Hope. It's great news. Well done," said Ruth. "Learning all those lines will be tough but we can help you."

"Yes, you'll have to work really hard!" said Charity, wagging a finger at her sister, but smiling at the same time.

"I will, I promise!" said Hope.

"What part does Merry have?" asked Gabrielle, looking at Sylvie.

"Penelope Pomander," said Sylvie.

"Oh, that's good," said Gabrielle. "In fact, I must go and see how Merry is," she went on, knowing that her friend would also be disappointed about not being picked for Angelica.

She floated down the corridor and when she popped her head round the door of the

Silverlight dorm, Gabrielle saw Merry sitting on her bed looking glum, while Larissa and Fey tried to comfort her.

"Hey, Merry," Gabrielle called softly. She glided over and sat next to her on the bed. "Never mind, it'll be great fun pretending to be sisters, and we won't have as many lines to learn."

"Yeah, you're right," said Merry. "I thought I wasn't going to get it, but I was secretly hoping you would. I know you'd be really good!"

"Aw, that's sweet," said Gabrielle. "Let's just enjoy ourselves, shall we? And make the best of it – make Madame Seraph proud."

"Yes, you're right!" said Merry. "First rehearsal is in the morning, so let's have fun!"

"Exactly!" said Gabrielle with a smile.

Inside her, there was still a dull ache of disappointment, but she knew it would pass. This was her first school show at Angel Academy and, although she wasn't the star, she'd been given one of the biggest roles. *I'm really very lucky!* she decided.

Chapter 11

As soon as the cast list was settled, some normal lessons were suspended to allow the Cherubics more time to practise for the show. They would be performing it in front of their parents two days before the end of term, and as they were now well over halfway through the term, that didn't leave very much time at all.

*   *   *

Next morning, as they met in the theatre for the first rehearsal, there was a buzz of excitement in the air.

Once they were all assembled, Angel Fleur addressed the cast.

"This is a thrilling time for us all, Cherubics," she said. "But the show will only work out if everyone pulls together. Here are the full scripts. I suggest you highlight all your own lines in coloured pen and please make sure you know them by next week. I cannot stress enough just how important it is for you to learn your lines early on, otherwise things will go badly. I say this from past experience, girls! This may be your first school show, but it's certainly not mine!"

The Cherubics took out their coloured highlighter pens from their bags and began to highlight their own lines and any stage directions which related to them. As Hope sat for a lot longer than anyone else with her coloured pen, everyone could see just how many words she was going to have to learn.

"Oh dear," Hope wailed. "I've counted Angelica's lines."

"How many?" asked Gabrielle.

"674 lines in total!" she declared.

"Wow, that's a lot to learn," Gabrielle said, giving her friend a sympathetic smile.

Angel Fleur floated about between the stage and the auditorium, giving directions here, there and everywhere. She'd asked Charity to accompany her and take notes, and Charity's smile lit up her face as she followed the teacher with a notepad and pen, taking down everything that she was told.

Gabrielle realized that Ruth had been right when she said it would all be fine once everyone knew what they were doing.

While Angel Fleur took the key cast members through the first scene with Angel Lara at the piano, other girls sat in happy huddles practising their lines, and teachers and some of the more artistic Cherubics busily created the props and backdrop. This was Angel Academy at its best, and Gabrielle felt proud to be a part of it.

Charity was busily organizing everyone.

"She looks so happy!" said Gabrielle.

"Yes," agreed Hope. "That's my sister – never happier than when she's organizing things!"

Gabrielle wasn't required to run through her lines for a while, so she went backstage

to see what was going on there. Angel
Willow had set up in one of the dressing
rooms, and Gabrielle peered in curiously,
looking at rails of
wonderful, half-made
costumes, headwear and shoes.
She recognized some of the outfits
they had helped with on the previous
Friday. Angel Willow had drawings of all the
costumes on the walls and a
measuring tape around her neck
and was taking measurements of
various girls, scribbling the numbers on
a pad. When she saw Gabrielle, she smiled
warmly and waved at her. "It's chaos in
here!" she exclaimed. "But I'm loving it!"

"The costumes are going to be great!"
said Gabrielle enthusiastically.

Hope was already in there getting her costumes fitted first as she had the main role. Gabrielle felt a pang of wistfulness as she watched Hope being measured for Angelica's finale dress. The drawing of it looked adorable. It was long, white and floaty, trimmed with pearls and feathers, and finished with a shimmering train… Gabrielle would have loved to wear it, but she thought of her own words of advice to Merry and decided to work hard to make her role as Peaches Pomander a success.

Over the next two weeks, Gabrielle and the other Cherubics worked incredibly hard. If they weren't out in the grounds with Angel Leonora, practising their skills for the Messenger Charm test, or baking cakes with

Angel Honey, they were memorizing their lines for the show. They spent lots of time in the theatre, running through scenes, helping with finishing touches for the costumes, moving props around, trying out lighting, or otherwise generally being organized by Charity, who loved her role as director's assistant. Gabrielle was excited to be measured up for the outfits Peaches would wear, which were very cute: patterned tights, sweet dresses and lots of lovely beads.

Every time Gabrielle was in a costume fitting, she realized Hope was in there too, endlessly sketching ideas for Angelica's dresses, and sometimes stitching little beads onto one of her gowns. *It's almost as if Hope prefers making the costumes to the actual part itself – she spends more time sewing than learning her lines!* thought Gabrielle.

During one rehearsal covering the second act, Hope was busily trying on one of her costumes when she should have been onstage rehearsing. And once she got on the stage, Hope bumbled through her lines, getting most of them wrong.

Angel Fleur became a little annoyed. "Hope, have you *really* been trying to learn the lines?" she asked.

"Yes, I really have," said Hope. "But I can only focus for a few minutes, then my mind wanders. I had no idea I was this bad at memorizing!"

"Gabrielle, you've learned your lines. Do you think you could help Hope practise hers, please?" said Angel Fleur.

"Yes, Angel Fleur, of course," said Gabrielle. "Hope, let's do that back in Crystals."

"Well, okay, but I have another fitting for the finale dress, so maybe after that," said Hope.

Gabrielle felt a pang of concern. Although she'd got the main part, Hope just didn't seem to want to spend time preparing properly for it.

After tea, Gabrielle sat with Hope in Crystals.

"Okay, let's get on with your lines," said Gabrielle.

"Oh, do we have to?" said Hope. "I'm exhausted."

"Yes, we really must because I promised Angel Fleur. Come on, it could be fun!" said Gabrielle. "You say the line, then I'll say it, then you say it without looking at the script."

Hope sighed. Gabrielle had used this system with Ruth and Merry and found it very helpful – even now, the lines she was practising with Hope were beginning to lodge in her head. However, Hope was having difficulties concentrating. She kept getting up and flitting around the dorm.

"This is driving me nuts!" she declared. "I can't do it. I'll try again tomorrow after a good night's sleep!"

Gabrielle bit her lip. She hated to give up, but there was nothing she could do if Hope refused to cooperate.

Gabrielle found that memorizing lines for the show was good practice for learning to memorize messages for the charm test. However, the final Messenger Charm lesson before the test was very stressful.

"Today, we will test each other on fifteen-word messages," said Angel Leonora at the start of the lesson. "And anyone who has trouble with this, please let me know. I would not expect anyone to experience difficulties with remembering a few words now when you are all learning your lines for *Angelica* so brilliantly!"

Gabrielle caught Hope's eye.

Hope looked panicky. "Can I be your partner, Gabrielle?" she asked.

"Sure," said Gabrielle.

"Please don't tell Angel Leonora if I'm a bit shaky. It's because of the show," Hope whispered.

"Erm…but she did ask us to admit if we were finding it difficult…" said Gabrielle.

"Pleeease," begged Hope. "I can't bear the thought of another teacher telling me off!"

"Okay, but let's try really hard," said Gabrielle.

Each pair of Cherubics was given several different messages. They took it in turns to memorize them and then recite them to their partner.

Hope just couldn't recall the messages at all – but as Gabrielle had promised not to tell the teacher, there was nothing she could do. However, she worried that if Hope couldn't memorize messages for the test *or* her lines for the show, she was heading towards disaster!

Chapter 12

With just a few days to go, the rehearsals for *Angelica* were getting much more intense. They were close to a full dress rehearsal in front of the staff, the older girls and, of course, Madame Seraph. Gabrielle noticed that Angel Fleur was getting more and more stressed and became very unhappy if someone didn't know their lines.

Everyone had been making a lot of

excuses for Hope, as she had so many more lines to learn than the rest of the cast and she was a very friendly and popular Cherubic, so no one liked to see her struggling. But now that the show was just around the corner, Angel Fleur was losing her patience.

"Hope Honeychurch! You're still failing to string two lines together! It is outrageous at this point in the proceedings!" said the teacher crossly.

"I'm sorry. I have been trying," said Hope desperately. "And Gabrielle's been brilliant at helping. I'm afraid I just didn't realize how dreadful my memory truly is!"

"Well, if that really is the case, perhaps we have miscast you," said Angel Fleur.

"Please give me another chance to learn

the lines," begged Hope, gulping. "I promise I will concentrate on them tonight and I'll come back tomorrow word-perfect."

"Okay… But this is your last chance, Hope," said Angel Fleur. "I don't know if you're lazy or forgetful, but don't come back here until you know all the lines by heart."

Gabrielle was shocked to hear her favourite teacher's outburst. But she realized that there was a very good reason for it – if Hope didn't know her lines, the show would be ruined.

After the rehearsal, Gabrielle found Hope sobbing backstage.

"Oh, Gabrielle, I don't know why I took on this part. None of the lines stick in my head. I'm an idiot," said Hope.

"No, you're not," said Gabrielle kindly. "Some people have creative brains but maybe they don't have such good memories. Who cares? We'll sit here until we've got it sorted, okay? I was thinking, if I say all the other characters' lines, that should give you an idea of where to come in with your own."

"You're so kind," said Hope. "I will try. My mind just wanders, that's all."

Over the next few hours, Gabrielle and Hope worked endlessly on the lines for Angelica.

But Hope still struggled to recall them. "It's no good," she sighed. "What am I going to do?"

"We'll chant them!" suggested Gabrielle. "And I'll write the tricky ones on flash cards for you. It's got to be worth a try."

Hope nodded gratefully and they carried on working at it. But she kept making so many mistakes.

"I don't understand it," said Gabrielle, "you're brilliant at the songs! You sing them beautifully and you never forget the words!"

"Oh, I know the songs all right, I've been singing them since I was little," said Hope.

"Well, at least that's a good start. And I'm sure we can make the lines stick too. We just need to keep trying."

Charity brought them some bread, ham, cheese and grapes from the Ambroserie as there was no time to stop for tea. Towards the end of their private rehearsal, Gabrielle looked up and saw Angel Fleur watching them. She hoped their teacher knew just how hard Hope was trying.

* * *

By the next morning's rehearsal, Hope
was much, much better at her lines.

"Not quite perfect yet," said Angel Fleur,
smiling, "but a huge improvement. Well
done, Hope. And Gabrielle."

Hope beamed proudly and Gabrielle
smiled too. All that mattered to her was
that the show was the best it could be. And
she knew there wasn't long left to make it
that way.

It would have been easy for the drama of
the big show to make the Messenger Charm
seem less important, but the girls knew this
wasn't the case. The charm was the most
important thing in terms of their training
and progress at Angel Academy. Before they

knew it, it was the eve of the test, and they began to panic.

"I'm really worried about doing the test. We've been putting in so much time on the show that I'm not sure I'm ready!" said Gabrielle.

"How do you think I feel?" said Hope. "I've packed out my brain with lines for the show. I've got no room for memorizing other stuff!"

"The best thing for all of you," said Sylvie from the windowsill, "is to get a good night's sleep so that you're fresh for the morning."

"You're right, Sylvie," said Ruth. "There's nothing we can do now because we won't see the message until we get to the test. I'm going to have an early night!"

"Okay. Night then!" said Gabrielle, snuggling into her own cosy bed.

But as they all settled down, Gabrielle noticed that Hope was still going over lines for the show, reading her script with a torch, and looking very anxious.

Poor Hope, thought Gabrielle, as she fell into a fluffy cloud of sleep. *She really is trying at last. But what if it's too late?*

Chapter 13

It was the morning of the Messenger Charm test and the spring sun cascaded in the window of Crystals dorm. Gabrielle felt a flutter of nerves as she got dressed. *What if I can't find the message? What if I forget what it says?* These thoughts kept running through her mind, and she just wished that it was over and done with.

The four Cherubics from Crystals went to the Ambroserie together, where they had creamy porridge laced with juicy blueberries. The others chattered away nervously, but Hope was really quiet.

"Just think, by lunchtime it'll all be over!" said Ruth breezily.

"But the *show* won't be over!" said Hope, looking a little tearful. "It's the dress rehearsal this afternoon and the main performance tomorrow!"

"Oh, Hope, try not to panic. Take one thing at a time, that's what Domino always tells me," said Gabrielle.

"Well, I'm worried about baking for our parents later. It's now or never for those pesky cupcakes," said Ruth. "What a busy day this is going to be!"

After breakfast, they met Angel Leonora out on the lawns.

"Now, Cherubics," said Angel Leonora. "Today, as you know, is the test, and the same instructions apply as for all our previous lessons. Home in on an object and say the opening spell. Read the message, commit it to memory, say the exit words, then act on the message. Members of staff will be waiting for you at the kitchens, where we will ensure you can repeat your message word for word. Then you must be ready to make your cupcakes straight after the test. It's a very tight schedule today. Are there any questions?"

"Do we all get the same message?" asked Hope.

"That wouldn't really test your individual

skills," said Angel Leonora. "Occasionally, two people may get a similar message, but just concentrate on the one you're given and act on it. Don't worry about what anyone else is doing. Now quickly form a line, please."

The girls queued as they had done in practice sessions, and this time Gabrielle made sure she was near the front, just behind Hope, who seemed anxious to get the test over and done with.

Gabrielle wondered where her message would be located this time. She always felt a moment of panic when she said the spell, worrying that the message might not appear, so she reminded herself to stay calm. After a fidgety few moments in line, she got the go-ahead to set off.

She zoomed across the lawns, the angel dust in her halo pulling her towards the kitchen garden. The wind blew her hair back off her face and for a moment she forgot she was being tested and just enjoyed the sensation of being directed by this strong force. Then she found herself homing in on the herb garden by the kitchen windows. One particular lavender bush seemed to be tugging her towards it and she hovered over it. *Oh no! What am I supposed to say?* she thought. She took some deep breaths. Then it came to her and she said the well-rehearsed words.

"*Angel bright, Angel sight,*
Show the note, Make it float."

For a moment, nothing happened. But then, thankfully, the message materialized, sparkly words appearing in the air:

Gather green peppermint, lavender,
and pink rose petals too – icing cakes is fun
for you!

As Gabrielle chanted it over and
over to make sure she memorized
the message exactly, she had a
funny feeling that someone was behind
her. But when she looked round, no one
was there. *You're imagining things!* she
thought. *Calm down, Gabrielle!*

When she had the message word-perfect,
she said: "*Message clear, Have no fear.*" And
at that, the message floating above the
lavender bush vanished.

The next task was to act on the message,
so she went off in search of the herbs and
petals which would be used to make icing
for the cakes. Once again she had a strange

feeling that someone was following her, but apart from other Cherubics fluttering around the grounds collecting their own items, there was no one close by. Shaking her head at being so silly, she found what she needed, taking time to pick the very nicest rose petals, then headed to the kitchen.

"Oh, hi, Hope!" she said, as she saw Hope, looking a little out of breath, waiting by the kitchen door with herbs and petals much like her own. "Wow, it looks like you were asked to gather the same things as me – peppermint, lavender and rose petals!" said Gabrielle, smiling. "I suppose we'll need lots to decorate all those cakes."

"Erm, yes, suppose so…" said Hope. But Gabrielle noticed that she sounded rather vague and wouldn't look her in the eye.

Angel Leonora approached them, looking rather fierce. "Gabrielle, I will hear your message; then, Hope, I will deal with you!" she said.

Gabrielle was surprised at Angel Leonora's words. Whatever did she mean by "I will deal with you"?

Gabrielle managed to relate her message perfectly to Angel Leonora, who said the lovely words: "Gabrielle, I am happy to tell you that you have passed the Messenger Charm test. Now, head off to the baking kitchen, please."

Gabrielle floated off, but couldn't help overhearing a bit of what Angel Leonora was now saying to Hope. "I am so disappointed in you, Hope. How could you even consider cheating like that…?"

Gabrielle didn't hear Hope's response but she shuddered. To be accused of cheating at Angel Academy was one of the most serious things imaginable. What could Angel Leonora mean? What had Hope done?

Chapter 14

Ruth and Charity arrived at the baking kitchen one after the other, ashen-faced.

"Is Hope with you?" asked Gabrielle anxiously.

"No. We don't know what's going on. But she's in serious trouble!" said Charity, sounding very upset.

As she spoke, Sylvie appeared at the kitchen window. The little dove always seemed to know when the Crystals girls had a problem. It was one of the things that made her so adorable.

Charity rushed over to her. "Can you please find out what's happened to Hope?" she pleaded.

"I'll try," promised Sylvie. "I'll come back as soon as I can."

"Thank you so much!" Charity called after her as Sylvie fluttered away.

More Cherubics began to arrive in the kitchen and it seemed that everyone had passed the test. Some angels had been given messages asking them to bring fresh flowers for table decorations, while others had brought oranges and lemons from the glasshouse for making fresh juice for the parents' tea party. Others had boughs of blossom for decorating the theatre, and some had brought fresh honey and jams from the storehouse. But the odd thing was that it seemed to Gabrielle that no two girls had received an identical message. And yet Hope had gathered the exact same things as Gabrielle. Had something gone wrong? Had she been given the same message as Gabrielle by mistake?

The girls from Crystals looked anxiously over to the windowsill every few moments, hopeful that Sylvie would appear with news.

Meanwhile, Angel Honey arrived and they launched into making the final batch of iced cupcakes, which would be served to their parents the next day after the show.

As well as perfect sponges, they were also tasked with mixing creamy peppermint icing, plus glacé lavender and rose water icings.

"I have a special extra ingredient for you to add," said Angel Honey. "Angel sparkle! You can collect it from my desk, but please use it sparingly!"

But even the prospect of sparkly icing didn't cheer the girls up. Ruth was so upset about Hope that she didn't mess around at all and, as a result, managed to produce a respectable batch of cakes. "They're actually edible," she said disbelievingly.

At long last, Sylvie appeared on the kitchen windowsill.

Charity dashed across to her. "What's happened to Hope?" she asked.

"I'm afraid she's in quite a bit of trouble," said Sylvie sadly.

"What kind of trouble?" Gabrielle and Ruth crowded round to hear.

"Well, apparently she got mixed up about the message she read in the test and couldn't remember what she was supposed to collect…all she could think of was the last line of the show, which was obviously no help at all. So she panicked and followed Gabrielle, picked the same herbs and petals as her, and then dashed back and recited what she could remember of Gabrielle's message. Only, she didn't realize that Angel Leonora had given everyone a completely different message this time…and besides, Angel Leonora saw her cheating; hovering silently behind Gabrielle and then picking

the exact same things!" explained Sylvie
breathlessly.

"Oh no!" gasped Charity.

Gabrielle and Ruth looked at one another
in despair. This was very serious indeed.

"Is she going to be punished?" asked
Ruth.

"Well, she can't expect to get away with
cheating," said Sylvie.

At that moment, Angel Fleur arrived in
the kitchen. The Cherubics fell silent.

"Girls, I have a very serious
announcement to make. I'm afraid Hope
Honeychurch was caught cheating in the
Messenger Charm test and as a result
Madame Seraph has excluded her from the
show. As you know, we are due to perform
our dress rehearsal to the entire school later

today. We are thinking as fast as we can about a solution, but as Hope had the lead role it is a very difficult situation. It would be awful to disappoint everyone due to one girl's misdemeanour, but at the moment there seems to be no alternative other than to cancel the show." There was a shocked gasp from all the Cherubics. "Immediately after this lesson, please report to the theatre. We will need to discuss if anything can be done and make a final decision."

This was a disaster! None of the Cherubics said that they felt cross with Hope, but Gabrielle could feel that they were. What if all their hard work had been for nothing?

Chapter 15

Gabrielle and the other Cherubics quietly finished decorating their cupcakes and then flew as fast as their wings would take them down to the theatre.

Angel Fleur waited for them there with a very sad look on her face.

"Girls, the last thing I want to do is cancel the show, but I honestly can't think what else to do," she said, sounding almost heartbroken. "Our problem is that Hope had the biggest part and we cannot go on without an Angelica…"

There was a terrible hush as everyone tried to think of a way forward.

Gabrielle's brain went into overdrive. She and Merry were playing Peaches and Penelope Pomander, and they had practised together so much that she was sure Merry knew Peaches' lines as well as her own. And she knew that Fey had been helping Merry learn the part of Penelope. So if Fey could be Penelope, and Merry could be Peaches, that meant…

But am I up to it? thought Gabrielle.

"Please, pleeeease, pleeeease don't cancel the show, Angel Fleur!" begged Ruth. "There *has* to be a way."

Charity put her hand up, looking slightly embarrassed. "I have an idea," she said, "though I don't know if everyone will go along with it."

"Go on, dear," said Angel Fleur encouragingly. "Tell us what it is."

"Well, Gabrielle has spent ages helping Hope with her lines and she knows the role of Angelica just as well as she knows how to play Peaches. I've heard her. Couldn't she be Angelica?"

Gabrielle gasped. It was as if Charity had read her mind! But could she really do it? What if she messed it up, like she had in the audition?

Merry's hand shot up. "I'm sure I could be Peaches!" she said enthusiastically. "I know all the words. And Fey could be Penelope…"

Fey agreed. "Yes, I don't mind. It'll take me a couple of hours to make sure I can remember all of Penelope's lines, but I know most of them already," she said.

"That could really work!" Ruth chipped in eagerly.

Angel Fleur's face lifted a little. "What do you think, Gabrielle? Would you consider it?"

Gabrielle blushed bright red, feeling a mixture of excitement and embarrassment. "Erm, well, yes, it's true I do know all of Angelica's words…"

A hubbub of conversation broke out as the girls all started talking at once.

"Give me a few moments to discuss this with Madame Seraph," Angel Fleur said. "Wait here. I'll be back as soon as I can."

The girls fidgeted as they sat in the plush red theatre seats. It was impossible to think about anything else while they waited for the decision.

After what seemed like an age, Angel Fleur returned. She looked happier. Could it be that the show was back on?

Chapter 16

"I've had a discussion with Madame Seraph," Angel Fleur said. "And we agree that Charity's plan might just work. Thank you, Charity – and of course a huge thank you to Gabrielle, Merry and Fey. It's great that you all know the lines so well."

"Hurrah!" cried all the Cherubics at once and they began to dance around, hugging each other.

"Now, we will delay the dress rehearsal for a short while to give everyone time to get familiar with their new roles," Angel Fleur went on. "I want you all to go and have a quick lunch in the Ambroserie, then I'd like the main characters onstage for a short run-through of the key scenes. Everyone else will need to go with Angel Lara to rehearse the dances and chorus lines. Then we'll meet back here for the dress rehearsal with full make-up and costumes. I'm sorry that our first proper run-though with the new cast will be in front of the whole school, but I just know we can do it!"

The girls rushed off to the Ambroserie, chattering excitedly. "This is the best news!" said Merry.

"I'm soooo excited!" said Fey. "I always wanted to be one of the sisters!"

As soon as they'd eaten and returned to the theatre, Gabrielle and the others went up onstage to start the rehearsal in their new roles. They worked with a will, but the Crystals girls couldn't help thinking of poor Hope. They hadn't seen her since the test – they hadn't had time to go and find her at lunch – and they were worried about her. It didn't feel right to be this excited when she was in trouble and suffering somewhere.

After they'd rehearsed the key scenes, Angel Fleur gave them a short break and Gabrielle suggested they go back to Crystals to see if Hope was there. The others quickly agreed.

When they arrived back at the dorm, Hope was gazing forlornly out of the window. But she smiled when she saw them and immediately hugged her sister.

"I'm so sorry. I've been such an idiot! Is the show completely spoiled because of me?" she asked.

"No, it's going to be okay," said Charity. "We thought of a plan. Gabrielle's going to be Angelica!"

"Oh, that's brilliant. I've been so worried about ruining the show for everyone!" said Hope. "That's been the worst feeling ever. I'm so relieved."

"Are you allowed to even help with the show?" asked Ruth.

"I've got to retake the Messenger Charm test later, and if I pass then I can be a helper, but obviously not the star," Hope replied.

"It's such bad luck for you!" said Gabrielle. "You had done so well with learning the lines."

"But I've forgotten them already!" said Hope. "I just don't have that sort of a memory. I should have admitted to Angel Fleur that I couldn't cope with it all – I realize that now. But you know the part so well, Gabrielle, you won't let anyone down."

Gabrielle began to feel very nervous about the responsibility she had taken on. She felt the weight of the school's expectations and remembered that her parents would be coming to see her too.

"I think I should go and read through the lines once more," she said. "I'll meet everyone down at the stage!"

Gabrielle flew off to the library and spent a while tucked away there, just saying the lines quietly to herself. But very soon she was out of time.

Okay, time to try this out for real! she thought as she headed off to meet the others at the theatre.

Everyone had been assigned dressing rooms backstage and Angel Fleur ushered Gabrielle into the one she'd be sharing with the other key members of the cast.

"Wow!" said Gabrielle as she saw the fabulous gold mirrors, edged with sparkling pink lights, and the fancy dressing table, groaning with the weight of bottles of perfume, make-up and hair accessories. "It's all so lovely," she gasped.

On the walls were pictures from previous shows, and Gabrielle felt honoured that she might be seen on these same walls by future Cherubics. The dress she would wear as Angelica for the finale was ready and hanging on the front of a wardrobe. Luckily Gabrielle and Hope were much the same size, so Angel Willow hadn't needed to adjust it. It was every bit as gorgeous as it had looked in the original picture. Floating, shimmering…perfect.

Angel Bellissima arrived to do the girls' make-up. Angel Honey brought snacks and drinks, and soon after that, Angel Fleur came in to check on them. Everyone was making such a fuss of them. In Gabrielle's case, this made her feel the heavy sense of responsibility once again – she didn't want to let Angel Academy down.

"I'll do my best!" she assured Angel Fleur.

"I know that, Gabrielle," her teacher replied. "I'm sure you'll make all of us and your parents very proud."

"I hope so. I'm dying for them to see me in the lead role. I wrote to say I was going to be Peaches, so this will be a complete surprise."

As Gabrielle finished getting ready, she heard a commotion outside and went to investigate.

It was Hope!

"I passed the test and I'm allowed to help

out!" said Hope. "Oh, Angel Fleur, I'm so sorry about what I did! I'm more relaxed already. I just couldn't cope."

"Oh, Hope, I'm sorry too. I should have realized that you were struggling and relieved you of the role much sooner," said Angel Fleur.

"Is it all right if I help Charity now?" asked Hope.

"That would be wonderful," said Angel Fleur. "Your sister is doing a fantastic job, but there is such a lot to do."

"This is brilliant!" said Gabrielle, hugging Hope. "I'm so pleased you're here. We've missed you."

It was almost time for the dress rehearsal to begin and Gabrielle was ready in Angelica's costume for Act One. She tried

not to worry as she prepared to perform the
entire show with no script to look at, only
the prompter in the corner. *Stay calm,
Gabrielle. The whole Academy is behind you,*
she told herself.

"This part is made for you!" said Ruth.
"Good luck!"

"I'm so proud of you," said Merry.

"Best of luck!" said Charity, squeezing
her hand.

"You deserve it, Gabrielle," said Hope,
giving Gabrielle a warm hug.

"Thanks, everyone, and
good luck to you all too!"
said Gabrielle.

Just before she took her
position on the spotlit stage, a strange
calmness came over her. The whole show

depended on her getting this right, but somehow that pressure worked well for her. It wasn't as if she was competing with her friends for the part this time. She *was* Angelica.

"Okay, let's go out there!" said Angel Fleur. "Good luck, everyone."

As Gabrielle floated onto the stage and looked at the back of the red velvet curtain, she thought about all the girls in the pictures in the dressing room who had done this before her.

She could hear the low murmur of hushed voices. The rest of the school must already be sitting in the theatre.

Her breathing got faster as the orchestra struck up with the opening number. *Just be Angelica,* she said to herself. *Don't think about it too much!* The curtain went up and the first song came to Gabrielle's lips quite naturally. She saw Angel Fleur smiling in the wings. It was a lovely feeling and suddenly Gabrielle *knew* she could do this…

She sang, danced and acted her way through the show with just the right amount of emotion. And although her sadness for Angelica came through powerfully in her performance, she didn't allow it to get the better of her this time.

At the end of the show, the whole school rose up from their seats and applauded for what seemed like an eternity. But it wasn't just Gabrielle who had shone. Merry and Fey had stepped into their roles brilliantly too. The school show was very much back on!

Angel Fleur was delighted. "I can't believe it!" she exclaimed between curtain calls. "You were marvellous, Gabrielle! I am so grateful to you! To all of you – you were superb."

After curtain down, there was a huge cheer from the Cherubics, and then a group of them came over to hug Gabrielle.

"I always knew you could do it," said Ruth.

Hope looked a little sad, but she was relieved too. "Thanks so much for taking over, Gabrielle," she said. "I just wish I'd given up the part sooner. I could sing the songs, but I just couldn't remember all those lines! I'm sorry. And I'm sorry about cheating too! I feel terrible."

"It's okay," said Gabrielle. "You got in a panic, that's all. It's a lot of pressure having all these things at once. I wish it hadn't been so awful for you, but I admit I loved it up there tonight! You did me a favour, honestly."

Although she was very excited, Gabrielle felt sleepy. What a day it had been! She needed an early night. And so, after a light tea, the Cherubics went off to bed.

Chapter 17

The next day began peacefully for Gabrielle. She had slept well and, as a special treat because they had been so busy the day before, Madame Seraph had decided that breakfast would be taken to the dorms for the Cherubics.

Four trays were delivered to the Crystals dorm, each with a glass of fresh orange juice, lightly buttered toast, a soft-boiled egg, and a chocolate twist croissant to finish. Gabrielle glanced at the calendar on her bedside cabinet. It was a big day ahead: first her parents would be arriving, then there was the school show, and that would be followed by the Charm-giving Ceremony. Seeing her mum and dad again was going to be thrilling– and she couldn't believe they were going to see her play the part of Angelica.

After breakfast Gabrielle headed to the theatre and ran through some of her trickier lines again. She wanted to do an even better job than she'd done in the dress rehearsal. She danced the awkward steps and sang the difficult notes in the dressing room. After that, there was nothing more she could do.

She ate lunch with her friends quickly and then dashed outside so that she could be on the lawns to greet her parents when Domino brought them in from earth.

It wasn't long before she spotted a dot in the sky growing bigger. She watched eagerly as her chevalange flew closer and closer, and then soared down gracefully to land in front of her. Mum and Dad immediately jumped down, and ran towards her with arms outstretched.

As Gabrielle hugged them close, her eyes filled with happy tears.

"Hello, darling angel!" said Mum. "You look so well!"

"Hi, Mum. Hi, Dad," said Gabrielle, smiling broadly. "I'm so pleased to see you both!"

"We're really looking forward to the show," said Mum.

"I can hardly wait!" said Dad. "You're Peaches, aren't you?"

"Mmm, I have a part," Gabrielle said mysteriously. "Make sure you sit in the front row!"

While all the parents went off to meet Madame Seraph and the other teachers, the Cherubics headed to their dressing rooms. Soon it was time for the show to begin.

As the curtains swished back, Gabrielle saw that Mum and Dad were sitting in the front row as she'd asked. Madame Seraph was sitting next to them.

Gabrielle closed her eyes and then she

opened them again. This was it. She *was* Angelica.

She sang, danced and acted her heart out, confidence from the dress rehearsal pushing her performance to new heights. She shivered in the snowy scene and sang movingly about her wish for a mother and father. She felt tears forming in her eyes, but instead of letting them spill over, she used her feelings to make Angelica as convincing as she could.

When she came on at the end in her finale dress, Gabrielle glimpsed her mum's expression. She looked as though she would burst with pride! And when it was time to take the final bow, the applause went on for even longer than it had the day before.

Gabrielle knew she'd done a great job. All the Cherubics had.

As the applause finally faded, Madame Seraph appeared in the centre of the stage. A hush fell across the theatre.

"Parents, Cherubics, staff – how proud I am of Angel Academy after this magnificent annual show. Everyone was simply brilliant, but I must thank Gabrielle for stepping into the lead role at the last minute. The performances thrilled us all. Girls, I think you should take one more bow."

As all the cast members stepped forward, the applause was thunderous. Gabrielle saw her mum had tears rolling down her cheeks, but she was smiling and clapping at the same time.

Madame Seraph held up her hand and

gradually the applause died down once more. "Now it is my honour to give out the Messenger Charms to these wonderful girls, who have had an especially busy term. Please form a line, Cherubics," instructed Madame.

Gabrielle was thrilled that she would be collecting her new charm in Angelica's gorgeous finale dress. She waited patiently and when it was her turn she glanced at Mum and Dad, who were smiling from ear to ear, before stepping forward. She couldn't help beaming too as Madame Seraph attached the beautiful sparkling new charm to her bracelet. And moments later, she was pleased to hear a huge cheer from all the other Cherubics as Hope stepped forward to collect her own charm. *Oh*, sighed

Gabrielle. *Everything has turned out so well. Thankfully.*

Once all the young angels had received their charms, Madame Seraph addressed the parents once more. "Now, we'd like you all to take tea with us in the Ambroserie. Your very talented daughters have not only put on this amazing show but they've been baking as well. Their cupcakes look and taste scrumptious. Believe me, I've tested them," she finished with a smile.

The Ambroserie had been decorated with spring flowers for the occasion and the girls' cupcakes had been beautifully arranged on cake stands. The whole room sparkled and shone.

"Ooh," said Gabrielle's mum, "this looks amazing. And, darling, *you* were amazing! What a day this has been."

"Brilliant," said Dad. "I wouldn't have missed this for the world." They tucked into the cupcakes the Cherubics had made and chattered happily with the other parents, who seemed intrigued and delighted to meet them and wanted to hear all about life on earth.

Gabrielle and the Crystals Cherubics formed a happy and excited group as they too munched cupcakes and drank sparkling elderflower cordial.

As she gazed around at her friends, her parents, and the gorgeous Angel Academy itself, Gabrielle felt like the luckiest girl in the world. "Thank you," she said, hugging each of her friends tightly to her in turn.

"What for?" they all asked her, laughing as she released them.

"For being my friends and sharing all this with me. I've just had the most amazing time ever since I started at Angel Academy!"

"And we've got so much more ahead of us," Ruth said, squeezing her arm.

Gabrielle smiled, "I can't wait!"

THE END

Gabrielle loves her life at Angel Academy.
Collect all of the magical stories in this sparkling series:

Wings and Wishes

Gabrielle's been invited to a very special school
but her new friends have shimmering wings and
sparkling halos. Will she ever fit in?

ISBN 9781409538608

Secrets and Surprises

It's time for the Wintervale Fair, full of lovely
surprises. But why is Gabrielle's angel friend,
Merry, acting strangely?

ISBN 9781409538615

Friendship and Flowers

Gabrielle hopes her birthday will be extra-
special in the angel world, but her friends are
keeping secrets. Whatever's going on?

ISBN 9781409538622

If you enjoyed

ANGEL ACADEMY

you might also like:

Silverlake Fairy School

by
Elizabeth Lindsay

Unicorn Dreams

Lila longs to go to Silverlake Fairy School to learn
about wands, charms and fairy magic – but spoiled
Princess Bee Balm is set on ruining Lila's chances!
Luckily nothing can stop Lila from following
her dreams...

ISBN 9780746076804

Wands and Charms

It's Lila's first day at Silverlake Fairy School,
and she's delighted to receive her first fairy charm
and her own wand. But Lila quickly ends up
breaking the school rules when bossy Princess Bee
Balm gets her into trouble. Could Lila's
school days be numbered...?

ISBN 9780746076811

Ready to Fly

Lila and her friends love learning to fly at
Silverlake Fairy School. Their lessons in the
Flutter Tower are a little scary but fantastic fun.
Then someone plays a trick on Lila and she's
grounded. Only Princess Bee Balm would be so
mean. But how can Lila prove it?

ISBN 9780746090947

Stardust Surprise

Stardust is the most magical element in the
fairy world. Although the fairies are allowed
to experiment with it in lessons, stardust is so
powerful that they are forbidden to use it by
themselves. But Princess Bee Balm will stop
at nothing to boost her magic...

ISBN 9780746076828

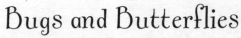

Bugs and Butterflies

Bugs and Butterflies is the magical game played
at Silverlake Fairy School. Lila dreams of being
picked to play for her clan's team, and she's in with
a chance too, until someone starts cheating. Princess
Bee Balm is also being unusually friendly to Lila…
so what's going on?

ISBN 9780746095324

Dancing Magic

It's the end of term at Silverlake Fairy School,
and Lila and her friends are practising to put on
a spectacular show. There's a wonderful surprise
in store for Lila too – one she didn't dare
dream was possible!

ISBN 9780746095331

For angels, fairies
and more sparkling stories visit:
www.usborne.com/fiction